ANATOLE
over Paris

ANATOLE
over Paris

by Eve Titus

pictures by Paul Galdone

McGRAW-HILL BOOK COMPANY
NEW YORK, TORONTO, LONDON

FOR MY SON RICHARD,
WITH LOVE UNLIMITED

In all France there was no mouse more famous than Anatole.

From midnight 'til dawn, unseen by human eyes,
he worked as Cheese Taster at the Duval Factory.

One day he found an old, torn giant of a kite on the boulevard.
Little did he dream that it spelled DANGER!

Tying it to his bicycle, he cried, "Finders Keepers!
My six charming children will shout with delight
at the sight of this mighty kite!"

And shout with delight they did—
first PAUL and PAULETTE,
then CLAUDE and CLAUDETTE,
then GEORGES and GEORGETTE.

His dear wife Doucette hugged him.
"Always your family is first in your heart!"

He patted her paw. "We'll patch a bit, we'll paste a bit,
and the old giant will look as good as new in no time.
Here's my good friend Gaston to help—let's work with a will!"

No sooner said than begun, and by late afternoon—done!

"Très bien!" said Anatole. "The kite deserves to be decorated. This I myself shall do, by painting little pictures of Paris."

The children played leapfrog at one end of the broad crossbar, while Doucette and Gaston sat watching at the other end.

Anatole, every inch the artist, painted happily away— the Louvre Museum, the Arch of Triumph, the Eiffel Tower—

AND THEN IT HAPPENED!

All at once,
from up out of nowhere,
there sprang
a great roaring lion of a wind!

Before anyone could say *"Jacques Robinson"* 7

the kite and its mice went up, Up, UP!

"HANG ON! HOLD TIGHT!"
commanded Anatole, and they did.

Past the chimneytops soared the kite,
past the tallest treetops,
sailing swiftly toward the sky,
dipping and diving and dancing about.

Then the roaring lion of a wind
became a playful puppy of a breeze,
and the kite climbed no more,
but swayed gently to and fro,
high above the heart of Paris.

Anatole ran up to the crossbar,
and there they sat,
nine mice with their heads in the clouds.

The children began to cry, and Anatole said,
"Forget your fears and dry your tears!
Does it matter whether we fly the kite,
or the kite flies us? *Non!*
The important thing is, we're together.
Maman will loop her long sash about you,
that you may sit more safely.
True, there is danger, but depend upon it—
Papa will find a way back to earth, and soon!"

"If your father says it, then it is so,"
declared Doucette, doing Anatole's bidding.
"How lucky you are to be up here!
You'll be the talk of the school. After all,
it is not every mouse who can fly over Paris!"

At that the children smiled, and stopped crying.

Anatole also smiled, but his heart was heavy indeed.

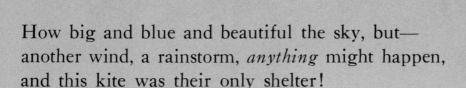

How big and blue and beautiful the sky, but—
another wind, a rainstorm, *anything* might happen,
and this kite was their only shelter!

So worried did he look that Gaston said softly,
"Are you not a mouse of much sense and many ideas?
You've managed before, you'll manage again—I'm sure of it!"

Anatole smiled. *"Merci, mon ami.* I shall do my best."

His eyes followed the passing parade of birds—
skylarks and sparrows and swallows and starlings, and others,
all too busy to notice the mice in distress.

He had heard that some birds eat mice, but he had no choice.
Remaining on the kite was by far the greater risk!

"*Attention!*" he said loudly. "I am the Captain of this kite!
Maman is mate, Gaston is lookout, the children are sailors.
With this breeze, we should reach ground by morning,
but warm beds are better than a chilly night on a kite.
One or two kind birds could land us now, before dark.
It is only fair that such goodness should be rewarded.
As the saying goes, *he who gives nothing, gets nothing.*"

He turned to the children. "Sailors, empty your pockets!"
"*Oui, mon Capitaine!*" Saluting smartly, they obeyed.

He inspected the curious collection—
two lollipops, four bottle tops, six lemon drops,
eight candy cats, and a squashed chocolate éclair.
He pointed to the éclair. "Perfect! What bird could resist?"
"BIRD A-H-O-Y! BIG BIRD A-H-O-Y!"
called Gaston from above.

Anatole hid the éclair behind him, his heart beating wildly.
Be it friend or foe—he was ready!

Soon a blackbird flew up, and stared in surprise.

"*Tiens!* I, Bonaparte, have seen many strange sights,
but—a kiteful of mice?   I can't believe my eyes!"

"You *can* believe your eyes," said Anatole earnestly.
"We're mice, all right—tired and hungry and homesick!
We need the help of a fine big bird like yourself,
who could so easily pull this kite back to earth.
It would be a good deed indeed!   Will you do it?"

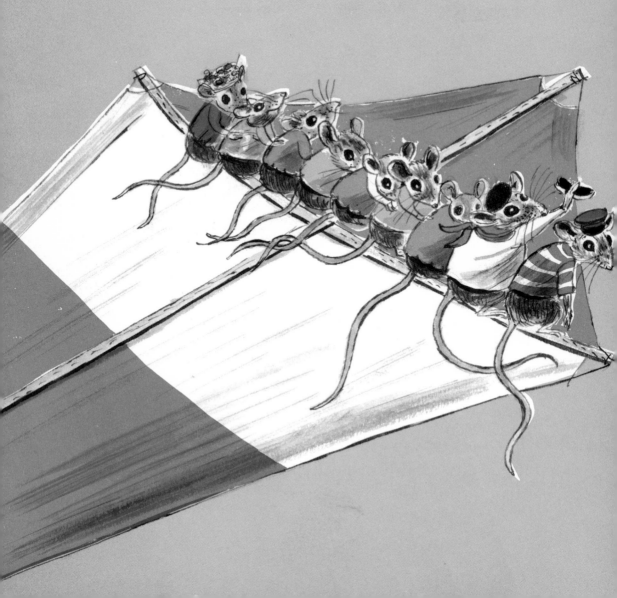

"*Non!*" replied Bonaparte rudely. "I happen to be in a hurry.
My wife's fixing my favorite dish tonight—Wiggly Worm Salad.
If I'm not home soon, my young ones will gobble it up.
Let somebody else help you! I must fly! Good-by!"

"Wait!" cried Anatole, waving the éclair in the air.
"Behold your reward!"

The bird's eyes bulged.
"Yum, yum! At your service, *M'sieu!*
I'll pull the kite, but I want my reward now, not later."

"Agreed," said Anatole. "But be sure to keep your promise!"

One greedy gulp, and the éclair was gone.

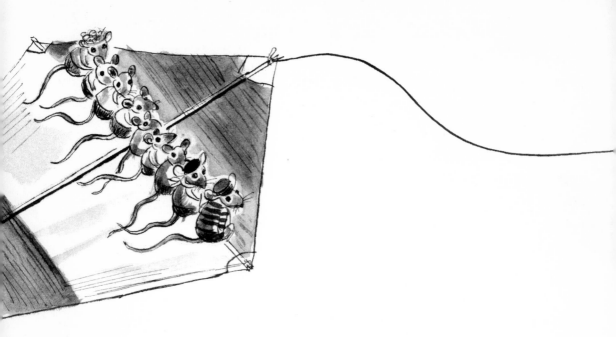

Then Bonaparte took the kitestring firmly in his strong beak.

Slowly but surely the kite was pulled downward,
slowly but surely the face of Paris appeared—
her fountains, her gardens, her blue River Seine,
and clearest of all, her Eiffel Tower,
standing tall in the scarlet sunset.

Upon spying the Tower, Bonaparte smiled slyly.

"The rascal's up to no good," guessed Anatole,
and he was right.

Down swooped Bonaparte at dizzying speed,
dumping the kiteful of mice on top of the Eiffel Tower!

"There!" said he. "Half a good deed is better than none.
What may be an éclair to a mouse is but a crumb to a bird.
If I hurry, I may still get my Wiggly Worm Salad."

"But what's to become of us?" asked Doucette. "Please don't go

Bonaparte shrugged. "Cheer up! Remember the old French sayin
one never goes so far as when one doesn't know where one is going
Or did Columbus first say this? Well, no matter.
Be glad I was pleased to meet you, not to eat you! *Adieu.*"

"Be a bird of your word," begged Anatole. "Finish the job!"

But it was no use—the flighty creature had flown.

"Birds, they're all alike," grumbled Gaston. "Featherheads!
As for the big brute who just abandoned us—
FEE, FIE, FO, FIDDLESTICKS !"

After that, they huddled together, as miserable as mice could b
and even Anatole wore a long face.

All were silent until Doucette said, "You'll save us, *cheri*.
How you will do it I do not know, but do it you will!"

Much encouraged, he replied, "My treasure, I shall try!"

He knew there were three ways down, none of them safe.
The elevators? They'd be crushed by the huge feet of people!
The birds?   He shuddered—what if the next one were hungry

The stairs? The Tower reached about a thousand feet up—
a hundred men on one another's shoulders would not stand as tall!
Clearly, so many steep steps were not for the little legs of mice.

Grownups might manage, but children would need to be carried.
A slip of a paw, a fall, and—again he shuddered.

Still, for the sake of his loved ones, he did not give up,
but kept the wheels of his mind churning and turning.

21

And at last his brain brought forth a bold and daring plan!
"*Voilà!* What a man makes of cloth,
a mouse may make of paper!"

Out came his knife, and he was everywhere on the kite at once,
slashing and gashing, ripping and snipping and clipping!

"Come now, have you lost your wits?" asked Gaston.
Then he guessed the reason, and cried, "He is a Master Mind!
Who but a genius like Anatole would think of parachutes?"

Soon they were wearing the finished parachutes,
after Anatole had tied all knots tightly.

At a nod from him,
they stepped to the edge of the Eiffel Tower,
face to face with space!

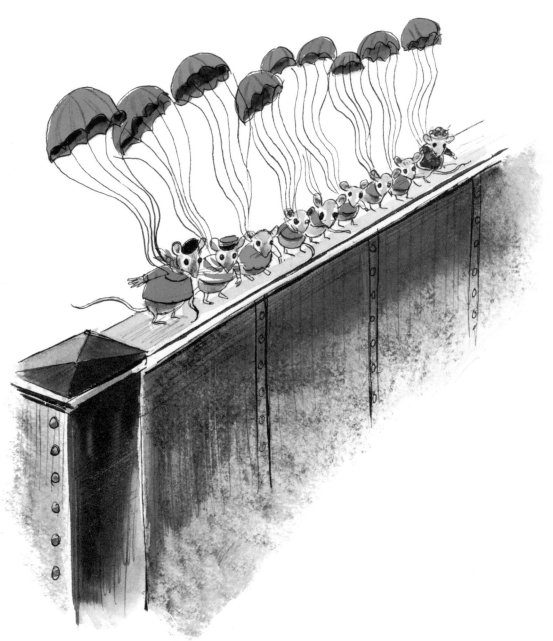

"*Vive la France!*" shouted Anatole, and leaped, and so did they!

The parachutes opened up like umbrellas, floating slowly down.

The sky had darkened to deepest purple,
and the lights of Paris were winking on, one by one,
like silvery stars.

"*Regardez!*" cried Anatole. "Ah, the beauty of it all!
I could paint a picture, I could write a book.
I could also sing songs in praise of France,
the home of the best of all possible cheeses!"

They were passing to the side of one of the Eiffel restaurants.
It was brightly lit, and crowded with people.

"I do hope they won't notice us," said Doucette anxiously.

Anatole laughed. "Only a cat could see us in this dim light."

But for once Anatole was wrong—they were seen by a man!
The man mistook them for what they were not, and shouted,
"Go back to Mars, you midgets—France is for the French!"

"Rubbish!" said his wife. "They're nothing but a pack of mice!"

Others rushed to the window to see what they could see.
Some sided with the husband, some with the wife,
and soon everybody was arguing with everybody else.

In the scuff and scuffle a waiter dropped his tray.
Frogs' legs flew here and there, slippery eels slid everywhere,
and some snail stew landed in the lap of a lady lawyer!

What a hullabaloo!   The diners couldn't dine,
the waiters couldn't wait, and the manager couldn't manage!
"Quiet! QUIET!" screamed the poor man.   But nobody heard.

"Are we Mice or Martians?" asked Anatole of the giggling mice.
"Such silly people!   Look—we're very near the ground."

But their troubles weren't yet over!

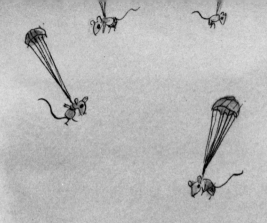

This time a wicked wolf of a wind picked up the little mice.
It huffed and it puffed, it howled and it yowled,
and it blew them far from the Eiffel before it vanished!

"Well," thought Anatole wearily,
"What next, on this day of surprising surprises?
The Statue of Liberty, perhaps?"

But there below them—who would believe it!—
was the roof garden of the Duval Cheese Factory!

They landed on the plump, rounded middle of M'sieu Duval,
who had fallen asleep while waiting for his wife.
Charlemagne, the good man's cat, napped on a chair nearby.

The sleepers did not stir, or skip a single snore,
for naturally, those who landed were as quiet as mice.

Anatole led the way downstairs to the big front door.
Easily squeezing their small selves under,
they stood upon good French soil again, at last!

Anatole rolled his eyes toward the skies. *"Quel voyage!"*

Then began a merry round of kissing.

"My dear Doucette!" cried Anatole, kissing her on both cheeks.
"My dear Anatole!" cried Gaston, kissing him on both cheeks.

"My dear Paulette!" cried Paul.
"My dear Claudette!" cried Claude.
"My dear Georgette!" cried Georges.

And so it went, with kiss after kiss after kiss after kiss!

Then Gaston said, "This hero of the air has saved us all!
He shall live forever in the hearts of his fellow-mice!
For Anatole there are three words—BRAINY, BRILLIANT, BRAVE!!!"

Standing on their heads, the children sang loudly and proudly,
OF THEE WE SQUEAK, MOUSE MAGNIFIQUE!

Some friends happened by, and offered them a lift home.
Two on a bicycle, all headed happily for the mouse village.

31

But that was not the end of the matter, for Anatole.

On the walls of a well-known mousehole,
in the Museum of the Louvre,
hangs a fine painting—*Sailors in the Sky*.

The artist? Anatole!

And in all France, from Calais to Marseilles,
the best-selling book among mice
is *Parachutes over Paris*.

The author? But of course—Anatole!

FINIS